# LONE WOLF and CUB

第 NO.9 巻

by

# KAZUO KOIKE

and

# GOSEKI KOJIMA

cover by

## FRANK MILLER

and

## LYNN VARLEY

小池一夫

小島剛夕

子連れ狼

FIRST PUBLISHING

Kazuo Koike
STORY

Goseki Kojima
ART

Frank Miller
COVER ILLUSTRATION & INTRODUCTION

David Lewis and Alex Wald
ENGLISH ADAPTATION

Willie Schubert
LETTERING

Paul Guinan
PRODUCTION

Rick Oliver
EDITOR

Rick Obadiah
PUBLISHER

Alex Wald
ART DIRECTOR

Kathy Kotsivas
OPERATIONS DIRECTOR

Rick Taylor
PRODUCTION MANAGER

Kurt Goldzung
SALES DIRECTOR

f you found this book on a shelf in your local Waldenbooks or B. Dalton's, nestled between the kind that don't have pictures or word balloons, you're probably unaware of the profound changes that have come to the world of American comics.

You might have run across a review of Art Spiegleman's *Maus* or Alan Moore's and Dave Gibbon's *Watchmen* in the literary section of your local newspaper. Or maybe you chanced upon a comics shop at your local shopping mall and noticed how many of the customers were adults.

Next time, go on inside the comics shop and take a look around. There's a lot to see, and you'll be surprised how much of it is worth a read. While most comic books are just what you remember from your childhood — floppy little pamphlets featuring the adventures of heroes in skin-tight costumes — some of them, more every year, sport square bindings, stiff covers, sophisticated graphics, and stories as literate and rewarding as you'll find anywhere. Ask the clerk to point them out to you.

Since they were first published some fifty years ago, comic books have been the quiet showcase for some extraordinary American artists and storytellers, and the uncredited source of ideas for wildly popular motion pictures. A generation of new artists and writers, inspired by these hidden treasures, has begun to bring new ideas of immense variety to the artform. Comic books have begun to grow up.

The same thing happened in Europe and Japan years ago, where comics are as likely to be written and read by adults as not. Consequently, much of the best you'll find, if you take my advice and look the situation over, are English language adaptations of comics from abroad.

You'll find Jean "Moebius" Giraud's visionary fantasy; Vittorio Giardini's subtle, complex tales of espionage; Lelong's hilarious bag lady Carmen Cru; Milo Manara's lush erotica; and much more.

*Lone Wolf and Cub* comes to us from Japan, where comics about everything imaginable sell in the millions to people of all ages. *Lone Wolf* is a nine thousand page epic adventure of a rogue samurai warrior on a violent mission of vengeance. It's also a fascinating exploration of Japanese religion and culture, and one of the finest examples of comic book art in the world.

That's right. Nine thousand pages. A nine thousand page comic book.

Don't be put off by its length, though. Each segment is a self-contained story, complete in its own right. You don't have to buy them all.

But you will.

Frank Miller
Los Angeles 1987

1626. THE THIRD YEAR OF THE KANEI PERIOD. THE *TOKUGAWA SHOGUNATE* COMMANDS THE CONSTRUCTION OF A *BELL TOWER* ON A PLOT IN THE THIRD BLOCK OF HONSEKI WARD IN *EDO.* IT IS TO BE 72 FEET BY 117 FEET. HOME TO THE *WAR BELL* OF THE TOKUGAWA, INSCRIBED WITH THE *HOLLYHOCK CREST* OF THE CLAN, REMOVED FROM THE WESTERN TOWER OF EDO CASTLE TO ITS NEW HOME.

THE BELL IS FIVE FEET TWO AND A HALF INCHES HIGH, THREE FEET ACROSS AT THE MOUTH. FOR YEARS THE BELL TOLLED THE *TIME,* ENABLING THE CITIZENS OF EDO FOR THE FIRST TIME TO LIVE BY THE HOURS OF THE DAY.

*EDO-- SITE OF MODERN-DAY TOKYO.

AS EDO GREW, *MORE BELL TOWERS* WERE BUILT ACROSS THE CITY, IN ASAKUASA, UENO YAMANOUCHI, HONJO, YOKOYAMACHO, SHIBAKIRI-TOSHI, ICHIGAYA HACHIMAN...

MEJIRO FUDO, AKASAKA TAMACHI, YOTSUYA... NINE BELL TOWERS.

FOR THE FIRST TIME, THE TOLLING OF THE BELLS COULD BE HEARD *THROUGH-OUT* ALL EDO.

FROM GENERATION TO GENERATION, THE *KEEPER* OF THE BELLS TOOK THE NAME *TSUJI GENSHICHI.* AS WARDEN OF THE BELLS, HE REIGNED OVER THE NINE BELL TOWERS OF EDO.

THE BELL TOWERS GUARDED BY THE TSUJI GENSHICHI WERE *BEYOND* THE LAW.

AND BECAUSE OF THE *VITAL ROLE* THEY PLAYED IN THE LIFE OF EDO, THE *AUTHORITY* INVESTED IN THEIR KEEPER WAS *GREAT*.

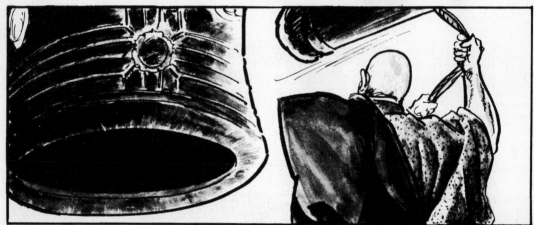

THE TSUJI GENSHICHI WAS
EMPOWERED TO COLLECT FROM
EVERY LAND- AND HOMEOWNER
IN EDO THREE *MON* *
A MONTH AS SUPPORT FOR THE
BELLS AND THEIR KEEPERS.
IN TOTAL, AN *ENORMOUS SUM.*
ENOUGH TO PAY FOR ALL HIS
SUBORDINATES, WITH MORE
THAN ENOUGH TO *SPARE...*

*MON--A SMALL COPPER COIN.

EH-HO! EH-HO! EH-HO!

EH-HO! EH-HO!

EH-HO!

MAKE WAY!
MAKE WAY!

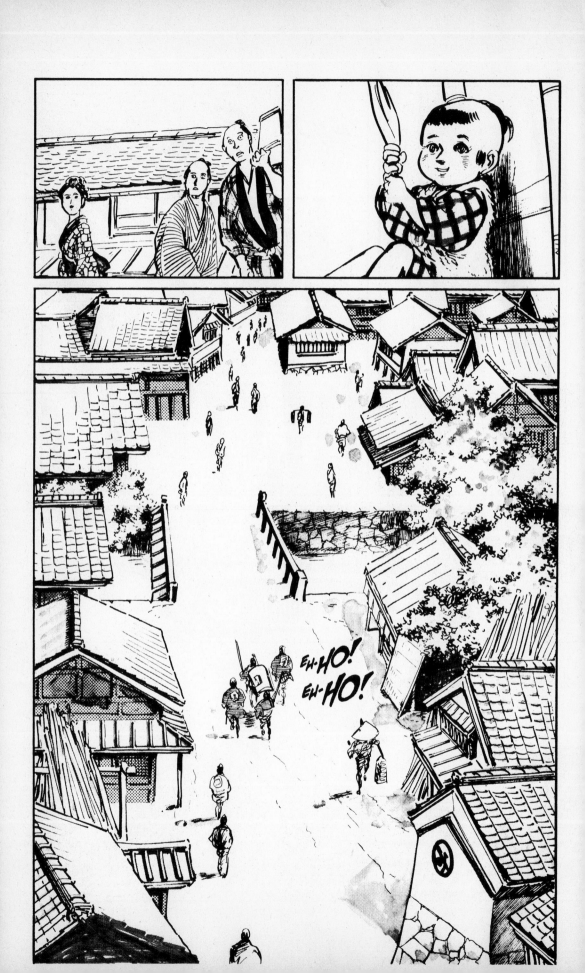

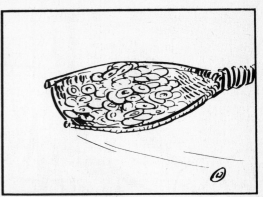

SSSSSH!

CLINK
CLINK

CHA-
CHAK!

16

WE HAVE RETURNED.

WHO'S THE BOY?

HE'S THE LONE WOLF'S CHILD...

WHY DIDN'T HE COME HIMSELF?

HE SAID IT'S ALL EXPLAINED IN THE BOY'S LETTER.

17

?!

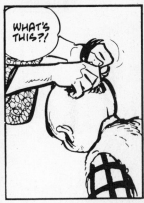

WHAT'S THIS?!

BY PLEDGE OF *HONOR,* I AM *FORBIDDEN* TO SET FOOT ON SOIL INSIDE THE *KUROBIKI.** I DESIRE TO MEET AT MACHIYA MIKAME ISLAND ON THE *SHUBIKI.*** I APOLOGIZE FOR ANY INCONVENIENCE...

READY A LIGHT PALANQUIN!

YES, SIR!

SO YOU'RE TO BE MY *GUIDE,* BOY? YOU'RE A *BOLD* CHILD.

*KUROBIKI-- BLACK LINE. THE LINE ON THE MAP INDICATING THE BOUNDARY OF THE EDO METROPOLITAN AREA. **SHUBIKI--RED LINE.

MAKE WAY, MAKE WAY!

EH-HO!    EH-HO!

EH-HO!
EH-HO!

EH-HO!
EH-HO!

KA-YONK

KA-YONK

KA-YONK

20

FROM GENERATION TO GENERATION, THE KEEPER OF THE BELLS HAS BEEN CALLED *TSUJI GENSHICHI.* I AM THE *FOURTH* BEARER OF THE NAME.

AS YOU KNOW, THIS BELL IS A *WAR BELL*. IT MUST BE *READY* TO BE RUNG AT ALL TIMES, EVEN IN DIREST *EMERGENCY*. ANY WHO WOULD SUCCEED ME MUST FIRST AND FOREMOST HAVE *HEART*!

SHOULD THE BELL TOWER BE A SEA OF FLAMES, SHOULD THE SKY RAIN BLOOD, HE MUST HAVE THE HEART TO RING THE BELL COOLLY AND CALMLY, SHOWING NO DISMAY!

NEXT IS *SKILL*. HE MUST HAVE THE TECHNIQUE TO PERFORM HIS DUTY, THOUGH HE MUST FIGHT HIS WAY THROUGH A THICKET OF SWORDS TO HIS POST. TO *DEFEND* THIS BELL IS TO DEFEND *EDO* ITSELF. A CRUCIAL POST, INDEED.

THUS WHOSOEVER WOULD BECOME THE *FIFTH* TSUJI GENSHICHI MUST *COMBINE* HEART AND SKILL IN A SINGLE BODY. HE MUST ENDURE THE GREATEST TRIALS.

SO TO BUSINESS... I WANT YOU TO *FIGHT* THE *THREE MEN* I HAVE MARKED AS *CANDIDATES* TO BECOME THE FIFTH IN OUR LINE. YOU ARE TO *CUT OFF* THEIR *RIGHT ARMS*.

FOR A BELL WARDEN, THE *LOSS* OF HIS RIGHT ARM IS THE LOSS OF HIS *LIFE*. EVEN SHOULD HIS LEFT ARM BE SEVERED, HIS TWO LEGS GONE, HE MUST BE *MAN* ENOUGH TO *PROTECT* HIS RIGHT ARM, AND TO *DESTROY* YOU.

AND IF ALL THREE LOSE THEIR RIGHT ARMS...

WHAT THEN?

THAT IS UNIMPORTANT NOW...

THEY ARE *NOT* YOUR *NORMAL* FIGHTERS. I SHOULD THINK YOU QUITE AN *EVEN* MATCH.

*IPPU* IS A MASTER OF *INJIUCHI*. *SHUMOKU* USES THE *MANRIKISA*, *GOBO* THE *SAJINRAI*. THEY WILL BE A CHALLENGE FOR YOU.

IF YOU HAVE ANY ADVANTAGE, PERHAPS IT IS YOUR *KILLER INSTINCT*, HONED ON COUNTLESS FIELDS OF SLAUGHTER.

CLAP. CLAP!

I ACCEPT.

1,500 *RYO*.* IS THIS ENOUGH?

23

*RYO -- GOLD MONEY.

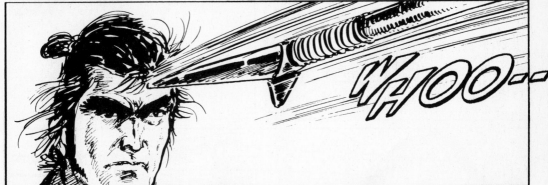

WHOO--

KLASK!

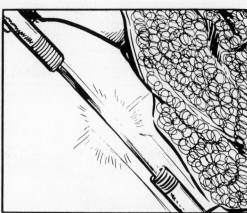

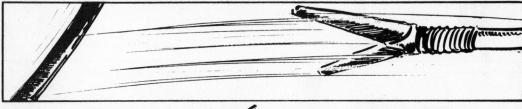

WHI-I-IP!

CLANK!

25

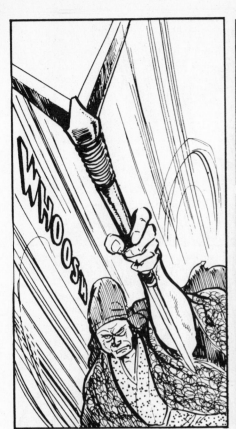

WHOOSH

SH-AK!

ERNG-NG!

26

TWACK!

MAGNIFICENT! YOUR SKILL IS EVERYTHING I EXPECTED. I'M IMPRESSED.

YOU *TURNED* THE STRENGTHS OF MY *KASEZUE* * TO YOUR ADVANTAGE TO SNAP OFF THE BLADES.

I PRESUMED YOU WERE HARD OF HEARING.

I-IT'S TRUE. LONG YEARS IN THE SERVICE OF THE BELL HAVE *DAMAGED* MY *HEARING.* I HEAR ALMOST NO SOUND.

I *READ* THE *LIPS* OF THOSE WITH WHOM I SPEAK. BUT NONE HAVE EVER CAUGHT ME. TELL ME-- WHAT GAVE ME AWAY?

I CAN TELL THE *VICTOR* IN ANY BATTLE FROM THE RING OF *DOTANUKI'S* ** BLADE. IF YOU COULD HEAR, YOU WOULD HAVE KNOWN THAT ANY BLADE MADE TO HIDE IN A STAFF WOULD FAIL YOU.

HMMM.

I HAVE MADE A *PROMISE,*† AND MAY NOT ENTER *EDO.* HAVE THE THREE COME TO ME.

CLICK!

*KASEZUE*--DEER STAFF.

**DOTANUKI*--THE NAME OF OGAMI'S SWORD. IT MEANS "PIERCES THICK TORSOS."

†SEE *LONE WOLF #1: THE ASSASSIN'S ROAD.*

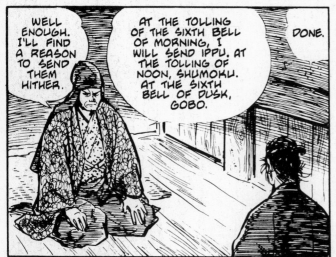

WELL ENOUGH. I'LL FIND A REASON TO SEND THEM HITHER.

AT THE TOLLING OF THE SIXTH BELL OF MORNING, I WILL SEND IPPU. AT THE TOLLING OF NOON, SHUMOKU. AT THE SIXTH BELL OF DUSK, GOBO.

DONE.

IF ANY *RETURN* BEFORE THE TOLLING OF THE NEXT BELL, I WILL ASSUME *YOU* HAVE BEEN DEFEATED.

FAREWELL.

29

AN ASSASSIN... IN *WAITING?*

30

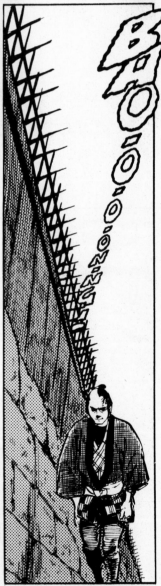

32

YOU ARE ITTO OGAMI...?

YES.

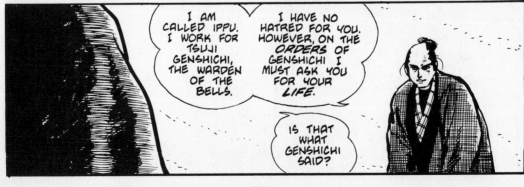

I AM CALLED IPPU. I WORK FOR TSUJI GENSHICHI, THE WARDEN OF THE BELLS.

I HAVE NO HATRED FOR YOU. HOWEVER, ON THE *ORDERS* OF GENSHICHI I MUST ASK YOU FOR YOUR *LIFE.*

IS THAT WHAT GENSHICHI SAID?

YES, SIR. I DO NOT KNOW THE REASON. I WAS ONLY TOLD TO FIND THE *RONIN*\* STAYING AT THE WATERWHEEL HUT ON MACHIYA MIKAME ISLAND.

HE SAID, "ITTO OGAMI IS HIS NAME. *KILL* HIM AND RETURN TO ME."

THEN LET US BEGIN.

KA-TONK!
KA-TONK!
KA-TONK!

HAVE YOU NO *WEAPON*?

I DO. LEST I BE CALLED A COWARD, ALLOW ME TO EXPLAIN.

I SPECIALIZE IN *INJIUCHI*.

SO GENSHICHI SAID.

\**RONIN*·· MASTERLESS SAMURAI.

34

WHAT!

FWEET!

THAT IS INJIUCHI.

I *DELIBERATELY* THREW *WIDE* OF THE *MARK* TO DEMONSTRATE.

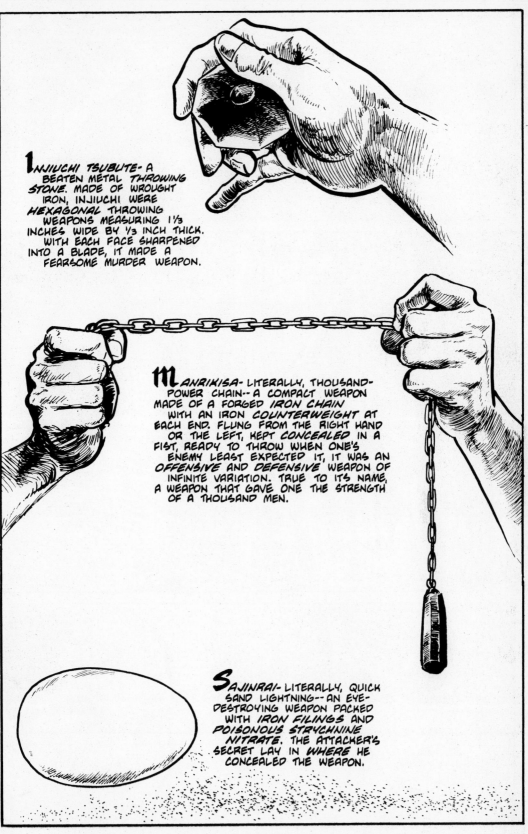

**I**NJIUCHI TSUBUTE- A BEATEN METAL *THROWING STONE*. MADE OF WROUGHT IRON, INJIUCHI WERE *HEXAGONAL* THROWING WEAPONS MEASURING 1⅓ INCHES WIDE BY ⅓ INCH THICK. WITH EACH FACE SHARPENED INTO A BLADE, IT MADE A FEARSOME MURDER WEAPON.

**M**ANRIKISA- LITERALLY, THOUSAND-POWER CHAIN-- A COMPACT WEAPON MADE OF A FORGED *IRON CHAIN* WITH AN IRON *COUNTERWEIGHT* AT EACH END. FLUNG FROM THE RIGHT HAND OR THE LEFT, KEPT *CONCEALED* IN A FIST, READY TO THROW WHEN ONE'S ENEMY LEAST EXPECTED IT, IT WAS AN *OFFENSIVE* AND *DEFENSIVE* WEAPON OF INFINITE VARIATION. TRUE TO ITS NAME, A WEAPON THAT GAVE ONE THE STRENGTH OF A THOUSAND MEN.

**S**AJINRAI- LITERALLY, QUICK SAND LIGHTNING-- AN EYE-DESTROYING WEAPON PACKED WITH *IRON FILINGS* AND *POISONOUS STRYCHNINE NITRATE*. THE ATTACKER'S SECRET LAY IN *WHERE* HE CONCEALED THE WEAPON.

FWOOO--

RRRRR!

CHAK!

CHAK!

FWOO--!

FWOO--!

S- SPLENDID...

THUD!

43

45

SO--
YOU'RE
ITTO
OGAMI.

THAT'S
ME.

I'M
GENSHICHI'S
MAN,
SHUMOKU.

HE TOLD
ME TO
KILL YOU--
SO HERE
I AM.

WELL--?

47

NOTHING PERSONAL, BUT YOU HAVE TO DIE.

WHAT THE BOSS SAYS, GOES.

LET'S GO!

THAD THAD THAD

48

TAP TAP TAP TAPTAPTAP

HYAAH!!

SHOOSH!!!

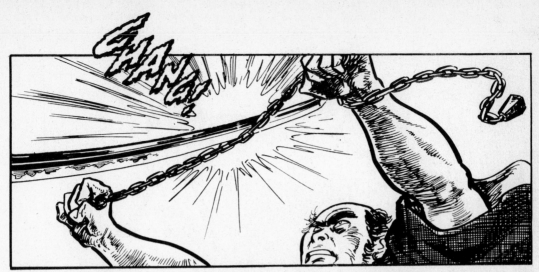

URNGH!

KA-TONK KA-TONK

:GASP!:

THUMP!

URE! KOFF! KOFF!

PAPA!

INJIUCHI AND MANRIKISA. THESE MEN WERE *MASTERS*, BUT NOT OF THE SAMURAI'S WORLD.

IT'S BEEN A FIRST FOR ME.

HE SAID THE THIRD MAN USES *SAJINRAI*!

WHAT WILL THIS BE?

SO YOU'RE THE GUY. YOU'RE THE RONIN THEY CALL ITTO OGAMI.

YES.

HOW DOES THE THOUGHT OF *3,000 RYO* HIT YOU? LET'S *DEAL.*

I'M JUST A BIT *SMARTER* THAN MY TWO OLDER BROTHERS, SEE.

WHAT!?

YOU KILLED MY BROTHERS, RIGHT? WHICH MEANS THERE'S NO ONE BUT *ME* LEFT. THE WARDENSHIP COMES MY WAY NOW. THERE'S NO *REASON* TO FIGHT YOU.

BELL WARDEN? MIGHT AS WELL CALL IT THE *MONEY* WARDEN, SO MUCH CASH COMES PILING IN! WE COLLECT *BELL FEES* FROM ALL OVER EDO! SO I'VE GOT A GREAT ESTATE COMING MY WAY. I CAN MAKE IT *5,000 RYO* EASY.

THE SIXTH BELL OF THE MORNING AND THE BELL AT NOON. MY BROTHERS WENT OFF AND NEVER CAME BACK. THEN THE SIXTH BELL OF EVENING'S MY TURN! ANYONE COULD GUESS WHAT'S GOING ON.

SO ALL THREE OF YOU WERE *BROTHERS.*

AN INCREDIBLY SKILLED ASSASSIN'S BEEN HIRED TO DECIDE THE FIFTH BELL WARDEN. AND THAT'S *YOU.* YOU *DID MY BROTHERS,* DIDN'T YOU?

MY FATHER'S OLD-FASHIONED.

WHAT DO YOU NEED A *TRIAL* FOR JUST TO *RING* A BELL? WE'RE NO SAMURAI. THE WORLD'S AT *PEACE*.

SO, HOW ABOUT IT?

NO!

SO YOU'RE GOING TO FIGHT NO MATTER WHAT.

WELL, IF YOU'RE THAT *EAGER* TO *DIE*...

THAT'S THE *PLEDGE* OF THE *ASSASSIN*.

HOW ARE YOU GOING TO STOP THIS MANY MEN SKILLED AT INJIUCHI? HA HA HA HA!

WITH MY BROTHERS DEAD AND THE WARDEN-SHIP MINE, I CAN USE OUR MEN AS I PLEASE.

KILL HIM!

POP!

ARGH!

GAK!

K-KR-GRH!

ARRGH!

K-K-

FWOOSH!!

YAARGH!

THUNK!

D-DAD!

FOOL!

WHY DON'T YOU *ABANDON* THE *ASSASSIN'S* WAY AND BECOME A BELL WARDEN?

NEVER!

CAN'T BE HELPED.

RINSE YOUR EYES IN WATER MIXED WITH *UNMO* CLAY. YOU SHOULD BE ABLE TO SEE AGAIN.

HOW COULD YOU SUBJECT YOUR OWN SONS TO A TRIAL LIKE THIS?!

IF THERE IS A WAY OF THE ASSASSIN, THEN THERE IS A *BLOODSTAINED* WAY OF THE KEEPER OF THE BELL.

EVEN YOU, IF YOU THOUGHT OF *YOUR* SON'S LIFE AND DEATH...

...YOU COULD *NEVER* FOLLOW THE ASSASSIN'S WAY.

IT WAS ALL I COULD DO TO SAVE MY OWN LIFE. NONE OF THEM LEFT ME ENOUGH LEEWAY TO MERELY SEVER THEIR ARMS.

I SAID IN THE BEGINNING THAT A BELL WARDEN'S RIGHT ARM *IS* HIS LIFE.

IT WAS ONLY THAT... AS A *PARENT...* I COULD NEVER ASK YOU TO TAKE THEIR *LIVES.*

IN ANY CASE...

62

THE *WARDENS* OF
THE BELL *VANISHED*
WITH THE DEATH OF
THE FOURTH TSUJI
GENSHICHI. LATER THE
TIME BELLS WERE
*REMOVED* TO TEMPLE
GROUNDS WHERE
THEY WERE TENDED
BY THE HANDS
OF *PRIESTS.*

## KAZUO KOIKE

**K**azuo Koike is considered to be one of Japan's most successful writers and a master scriptwriter for the graphic story genre. He is perhaps best known in the U.S. for his screenplay for the feature film "Shogun Assassin," a re-edited version of the Japanese film "Kozure Okami," based on the **Lone Wolf and Cub** stories. Mr. Koike currently operates a publishing/production company for comics, Studio Ship, Inc., which publishes the works of Japan's major comics writers and artists in both book and magazine format. Mr. Koike is also the founder of Gekiga-Sonjuko, a school which offers a two year course for aspiring professional artists and writers.

## GOSEKI KOJIMA

**G**oseki Kojima made his debut as a comic artist in 1967 with "Oboro-Junin-Cho." With his unique style Mr. Kojima created a new form of expressive visual interpretation for the graphic storytelling medium, and established for himself a position as a master craftsman with his ground-breaking work on **Lone Wolf and Cub**. Other works by Mr. Kojima in collaboration with Mr. Koike are "Kawaite Soro," "Kubikiri Asa," "Hanzo-No-Mon," "Tatamidori Kasajiro," "Do-Chi-Shi," and "Bohachi Bushido."

小池一夫　小島剛夕

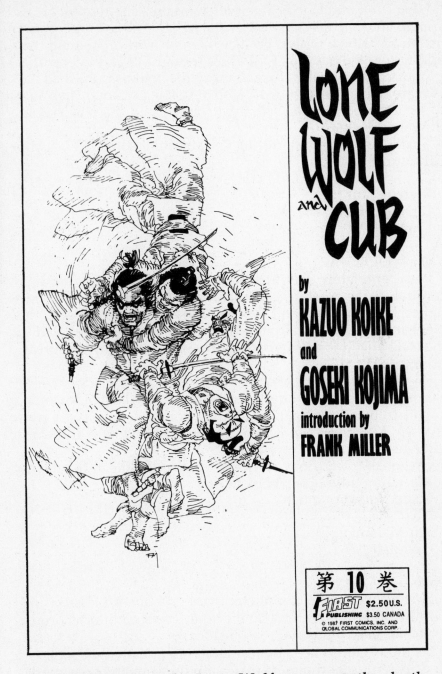

LONE WOLF and CUB

by

KAZUO KOIKE

and

GOSEKI KOJIMA

introduction by

FRANK MILLER

第 10 巻

FIRST PUBLISHING $2.50 U.S. $3.50 CANADA

© 1987 FIRST COMICS, INC. AND GLOBAL COMMUNICATIONS CORP.

Two children hire the Lone Wolf to avenge the death of their father at the hands of the "The Lawless Samurai." But *Bushido*, the code of the samurai, demands that the youths exact their own revenge, and Itto Ogami cannot violate the samurai code . . . or can he?

来月

Dear First:

Lone Wolf and Cub is an excellent series. The writing is superb, and the artwork brings out every emotion and scene of action Mr. Koike writes. Frank Miller's covers are a great addition to the book, as well as his thoughtful and interesting introductions. I really enjoy the way the book is published (square bound), real stylish! Also the price is a small amount to pay compared to other Japanese comics, and the material is definitely better!

Thank you for an interesting and different comic. I wish you continuing success.

Marcus Hui
Richmond, B.C.
Canada

Dear Mr. Oliver:

I am completely delighted that your company has decided to publish the masterpiece *Kozure Okami*. Being an avid fan of both Kazuo Koike and Goseki Kojima for several years, this is what I have been waiting for for many years. I am so glad that fellow comic enthusiasts are now able to enjoy this great book.

Responding to some of Lone Wolf and Cub's readers who think it should be in color, I must simply say that colorization of such a tremendous book would be a complete mistake! I know that Mr. Koike and Mr. Kojima would never allow you to do so; but I just had to show my view.

On behalf of all comic enthusiasts, I would like to thank you for bringing this superb book to us.

Thank you very much.

Kai Matsuda
Palmdale, CA

Folks:

First off, I'd like to compliment you on Lone Wolf and Cub For the price, it is the best comic book I read right now (and quite possibly the best in the business).

It's important to keep in mind that historically this book doesn't represent things as they actually were; in other words, this is a piece of fiction. What the book does represent superbly is the Japanese perception of conditions under the Shogunate. Itto Ogami encompasses many of the traditional perceptions of that period. A western equivalent can be found in TV cowboy movies; compare their image to what the west was truly like.

As all cultures do in their own fashion, the Japanese have idealized certain concepts and beliefs of the time, which have come to eventually represent Shogunate Japan in the minds of the Japanese; whether it is truth or not is irrelevant. Rightly so, as this is what good fiction is made of: hopes, dreams, and conceptions, not the cold, hard realities which history is actually composed of.

Hopefully, you all at First Comics are searching for more Japanese comics of the same caliber as Lone Wolf and Cub, as I would certainly be overjoyed at seeing more such books on the market.

Keep up the good work.

Chris Hutts
Spring, TX

*I might take exception to your comparison to cowboy movies. The Japanese are much more steeped in tradition than their western counterparts, and Koike and Kojima have taken great care to accurately reflect feudal Japan under the Shogunate. To be sure, many of the characters are somewhat larger than life — especially Itto Ogami — but the depiction of life, dress, and the samurai's rigid code of honor is far more accurate than your typical cowboy western.*

Dear Rick:
I would like to thank you and all others involved for bring Lone Wolf and  Cub to the American public. Many years ago, I saw *Lightning Swords of Death*, and more recently *Shogun Assassin*. I was very impressed. The violence was more detailed than the classic samurai movies (*Seven Samurai*, *Yojimbo*, and *Chusingura*), but the depiction of death is never pretty.

If possible, could you give me a list of all of the Lone Wolf and Cub movies, the Japanese title, year of release, and, of course, the star who played Itto Ogami?

Brian Paul Holiday
Stone Mountain, GA

*There have been six Japanese Lone Wolf and Cub movies under the collective title of "Sword of Vengeance." The first one was released in 1972. Itto Ogami was portrayed by Tomisaburo Wakayama in all six films. The original author, Kazuo Koike, also wrote the screenplays.*